My First Book of
SIGN LANGUAGE

illustrated by Joan Holub

Cartwheel
·B·O·O·K·S·®

SCHOLASTIC INC.

New York Toronto London Auckland Sydney
Mexico City New Delhi Hong Kong Buenos Aires

*With love for my
brother and sister,
Paul and Kristen*

ISBN 0-439-63582-9

Copyright © 1996 by Troll Communications L.L.C.
WhistleStop is an imprint and trademark of Troll Communications L.L.C.
All rights reserved.
Published by Scholastic Inc.
SCHOLASTIC, CARTWHEEL BOOKS, and associated logos are trademarks
and/or registered trademarks of Scholastic Inc.

Library of Congress Cataloging-in-Publication Data available

12 11 10 9 8 7   5 6 7 8 9/0

Printed in the U.S.A.   23

First Scholastic printing, February 2004

animal

apple

B

baby

bed

boy

car

cat

children

D

day

dog

drink

E

ear

eat

egg

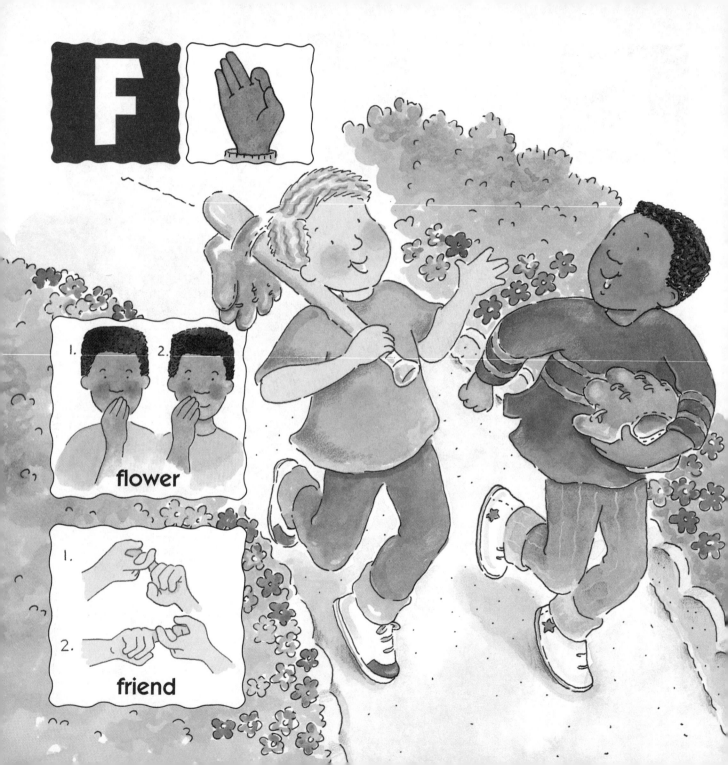

F

flower

friend

G

game

girl

green

house

horse

I

J

ice cream

jump

K

kid

kiss

kitchen

L

learn

library

light

M

man

monster

movie

night

noon

old

open

out

P

people

pizza

play

question

quiet

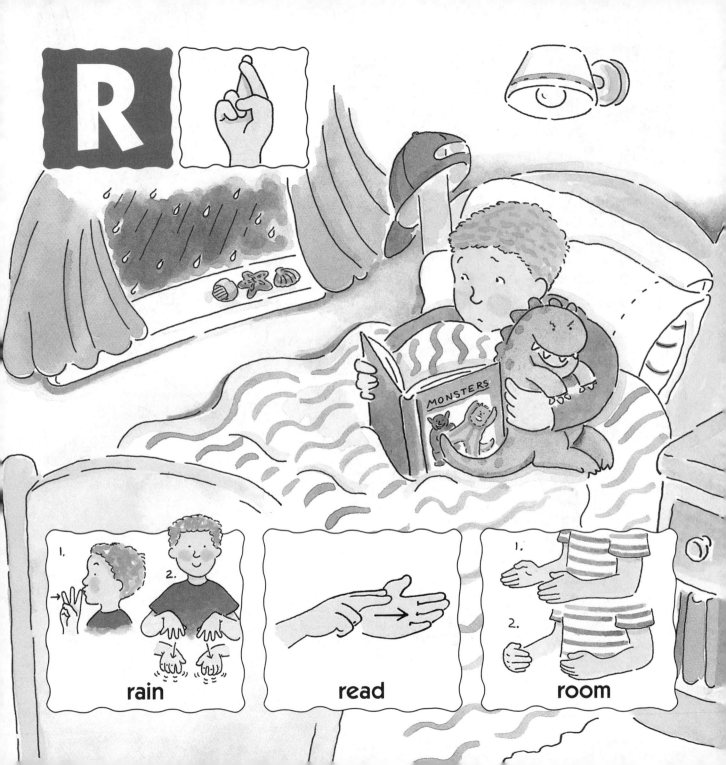

R

rain

read

room

S

school

scissors

sit

T

talk

television

tree

U

V

umbrella

up

vacation

W

walk

water

work

X **x** **Y** **y**

X - RAY

x-ray

yellow

zebra

zoo

More Helpful Signs

I

you

me

he

she

they

is

are

am

Family

mother

father

sister

brother

grandmother

grandfather

what

where

when

why

who

how

have

do

go

get

like

love

Counting

1

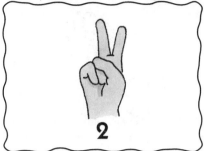

2

3

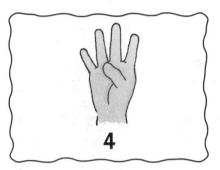

4

5

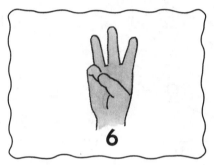

6

7

8

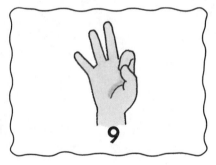

9

10

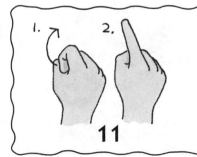

11

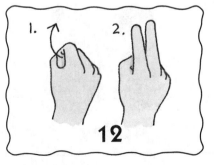

12

 **Sunday**

 **Monday**

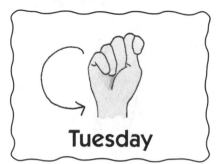 **Tuesday**

 **Wednesday**

 **Thursday**

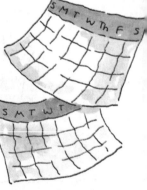

 **Friday**

 **Saturday**

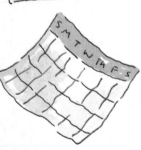

 **today**

 **tomorrow**

 **yesterday**

happy

sad

big

little

good

bad

hot

cold

please

thank you

you're welcome

I love you

sorry